D1371839

Retrieving with EVIE

by Susan Harp

Illustrated by Jon Siau

M.T. Publishing Company, Inc.
P.O. Box 6802
Evansville, Indiana 47719-6802
www.mtpublishing.com

Illustrations by Jon Siau.

The name and character of EVIE are property of Susan Harp. Rights granted to Keep Evansville Beautiful.

Special thanks to Fifth Third Bank for support of this project.

The materials were compiled and produced using available information. M.T. Publishing Company, Inc., Susan Harp, and Jon Siau regret they cannot assume liability for errors or omissions.

Graphic Design:
Alena L. Kiefer

Library of Congress Control Number:
2007900435

ISBN: 1-932439-67-6

Printed in the
United States of America

First Printing 2007
Second Printing, June 2009

Welcome to Labrador Lane! My name is EVIE and I want to share my story with you. I am a Yellow Labrador Retriever who lives with my human family in Evansville, Indiana.

Labrador Lane is located in a woods along Pigeon Creek. A lot of wildlife share my special place. Turtles, rabbits, squirrels, ducks, geese, foxes, deer, owls, and great blue herons keep me busy.

I like to swim in my very own lake and run all around my big yard, but sometimes I have to take obedience lessons. My daddy says I have to learn how to be a good citizen even though I am just a little puppy.

My daddy says I am a good girl and soooooo smart!

I can sit, stay, lie down, walk on a leash and retrieve. I love to retrieve best of all! Sometimes I show my wildlife friends the lessons I have learned.

One day my daddy took me down to the Ohio River. I got so excited when I saw all that water! I tried really hard not to jump in, but I just couldn't resist all those big sticks floating along the bank. I loved retrieving those sticks, but then something shiny bobbed up and down right in front of my nose.

Since I am so smart, I remembered what that shiny thing was. My family puts those shiny things into a big blue box. Yes, it was a soda can just like the ones my family recycles! I made my retrieve and took the prize to my daddy. He was very proud of me, but he said that I could cut my mouth trying to retrieve cans. He was telling me that we could take it home to recycle, but I had already plunged back into the river.

I couldn't believe my luck!

Soda cans were floating everywhere! I didn't know which one to grab first! Just then I heard my daddy say, "EVIE, you can't retrieve all those cans. We would be here all day and you could get hurt. Maybe some of our friends will help us retrieve these cans another day." I really didn't like leaving those cans, but I had to be a good citizen and obey my daddy.

It was lunch time so we drove up to one of those places that hands you a sack full of food out of a window. I love to stick my head out of the car and drool at those nice people! As we were leaving, I saw a man drop his yummy sack on the ground. I got so excited that I barked to let that man know I would gladly help retrieve his sack.

PICK-UP

11

As Daddy stopped the car to pick up the sack, I forgot my good girl manners. I jumped out and had that sack in my mouth before Daddy could get out of his seat belt. I looked all around for the man who dropped his sack. He was gone and to my surprise so was the food in the sack! I was really confused! My family always puts our empty sacks in the kitchen trash can at home. I am sure they do this so I can walk by and sniff for a few days.

Then I spotted two more sacks and wondered if the food was still in them. I looked around for the owners of the sacks because I was convinced these people didn't know their sacks were missing. Maybe they saw me retrieve the empty sack and wanted to leave me sacks with food. You know, I always did get special rewards in Obedience School for retrieving.

My thoughts were quickly interrupted as Daddy took the sack from my mouth. He threw it into a trash bin that was just a few steps away from where I found all of the sacks. "EVIE, you can't retrieve everything around this place. We would be here all day and you could get sick. Maybe some of our friends will help us retrieve these sacks another day."

I felt kind of sad as I hung my head out the window on our drive home. I love sniffing the air when we are driving on the Lloyd Expressway, but I kept thinking about all the things I didn't retrieve. I didn't understand why people would throw or drop things if they weren't playing retrieveeeee.

I felt a little better when some kids waved at me as their car passed us. Ouch!!!!! I felt a little sting on my nose and then it really started to hurt! I whimpered for a moment and then I just let out a howl. My daddy pulled over to see what had happened and he saw smoke coming from the car seat. I had been hit by a cigarette butt.

Those kids who waved at me were nice, but some adult in that car had thrown a cigarette out when they passed us. My daddy put some cool water on my nose and he said my fur was going to be okay.

I didn't feel like sniffing any more air until we got to Labrador Lane. I knew I wouldn't have to worry about Litter Bugs throwing fire at me once I got home. The only kind of bugs and fire would be from the fireflies that I liked to chase in my backyard.

That night before bedtime, my daddy said he had been thinking about what a good citizen I was. I had tried to retrieve the trash people had left, but it was more litter than I could ever retrieve alone. He said, "EVIE, let's call our friends at Keep Evansville Beautiful and together we can spread the word."

My daddy and I were both wagging our tails and dancing around the room. As we were dancing, my daddy gave a cheer, "EVIE, E...V...I...E," but then he stopped because he had another great idea. "EVIE, your name can send a message to our friends."

E - every

V - volunteer

I - is

E - essential

in keeping Evansville beautiful.

Now I know why I am soooooo smart, I'm Daddy's little girl!

Help EVIE retrieve litter.

Keep Evansville Beautiful!

How you can help....

Some tips from Keep Evansville Beautiful.

A "community" is any place that you and others are. Your classroom, school yard, playground and neighborhood are all communities.

A "citizen" is any person in the community, like you, your family, friends or neighbors.

Being a good *citizen* means taking responsibility for your *community*. We all must work to be good citizens and to be proud of our community.

Sometimes that means picking up litter that you did not drop. It means retrieving like EVIE. Being a good citizen always means not littering and reminding others not to litter.

Steps to help EVIE retrieve litter:

1. Wear sturdy, closed toe shoes so you do not slip or get cut.
2. Wear work gloves so you do not get cut or dirty. You can get gloves from Keep Evansville Beautiful.
3. Wear a hat to protect your head from the sun and from branches or thorny bushes.
4. Wear a long sleeve shirt and pants, especially if you are picking up litter in tall grass.
5. **SAFETY FIRST:** stay away from traffic, never ever pick up anything sharp and ALWAYS tell an adult that you are going to pick up litter before starting your work.
6. Get a good trash bag and have fun!
7. When you are done picking up litter, put the trash bag in a trash container for the waste haulers to pick up.
   GOOD JOB!

About the illustrator...

Jon Siau has taught art in Evansville, Indiana, at North High School since 1971. He has been awarded numerous awards and honors for his teaching. Twice Jon has won Evansville's "Teacher of the Year" award, in addition to two state honors, and three national teaching awards. In 1999, USA Today selected Jon to the All-USA Today Teaching Team. He was the only art teacher so selected. At a gala banquet held at the National Gallery of Art in Washington, D.C., the artist was honored with a national award for his work teaching students with learning disabilities.

In 2004, he received the Excellence in Education Award at Conseco Fieldhouse in front of an audience of 16,000. In 2006, Jon received the statewide and national "No Child Left Behind" American Star of Teaching Award. This award honored Jon as the top educator in the state of Indiana, from a field of 60,000 teachers. He was the only art teacher in the nation to receive this award.

Jon has shared his talents by creating artwork for such charities as: Keep Evansville Beautiful (formerly Operation City Beautiful), the United Way, Goodwill Industries and WNIN. His art can be found in all 50 states as well as France, England, Hong Kong, Japan, and the Virgin Islands. The United States Olympic Committee chose Jon to be its first commissioned artist for its international publication, "The Olympian."

About the author...

Susan Harp is a teacher at Dexter Elementary in Evansville, Indiana. She began her teaching career in 1978 and has taught Kindergartners for the last 26 years.

Susan and her husband Steve are active volunteers in their neighborhood and community. They received the Adopt-A-Spot of the Year Award from Keep Evansville Beautiful in 2003 and again in 2006. Through their efforts, beginning in 2001, with Keep Evansville Beautiful in the Adopt-a-Spot and Great American Cleanup campaigns, they became aware that more volunteers were needed to keep the community beautiful.

Susan knew that educating young students was a vital component in her efforts to get more people involved in the community. The EVIE character was created by Susan as a mascot that would appeal to all age levels.

The Harps have trained, shown, and been owned by numerous Yellow Labradors since 1977. They believe dogs have the ability to bring out the best in people. The Harps are currently owners of four Yellow Labs who live at Labrador Lane, a Certified Backyard Habitat with the National Wildlife Federation.

About Keep Evansville Beautiful...

Keep Evansville Beautiful is a privately funded not-for-profit agency that works to promote self-responsibility for a clean and attractive community. Founded in the mid-1970s, the agency runs local Adopt-A-Spot and Business Landscape programs; the annual Great American Cleanup during April, May and June; and coordinates and advocates for anti-litter education and civic beautification. KEB offers several innovative, hands-on civics education programs, with help from our sponsors, to local schools as we work to teach good citizenship to students and their families.

Keep Evansville Beautiful believes that self-responsibility is the key to a clean, beautiful and healthy community.

Check us out at *www.keepevansvillebeautiful.org*.
Be sure to visit the School Programs pages!

Special thanks to....

Fifth Third Bank has a history of excellence in community partnerships, and its enthusiastic underwriting of the *Retrieving with EVIE* program is another fine example.

Fifth Third Bank has been helping people pursue their dreams for nearly 150 years. Because of that commitment to help, Fifth Third has been recognized in Businessweek magazine as one of America's Most Philanthropic Companies. Its collaboration with Keep Evansville Beautiful, and other worthwhile organizations, only reinforces the national recognition.

The employees of Fifth Third Bank believe that by supporting important educational programs, such as *Retrieving with EVIE*, they can help our community meet today's needs while building a better tomorrow.

Thank you Fifth Third, from Keep Evansville Beautiful and all of EVIE's helpers!